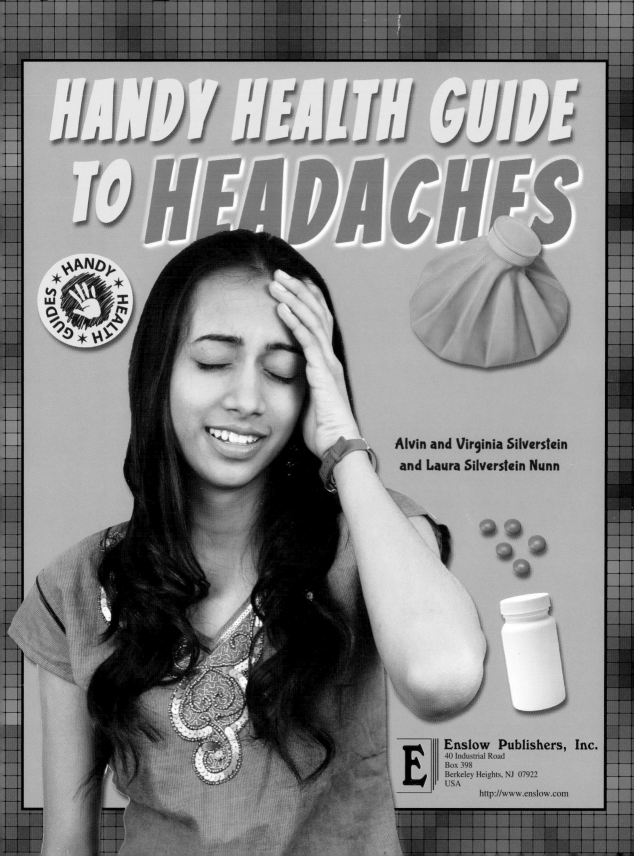

HANDY HEALTH GUIDE TO HEADACHES

Alvin and Virginia Silverstein
and Laura Silverstein Nunn

E Enslow Publishers, Inc.
40 Industrial Road
Box 398
Berkeley Heights, NJ 07922
USA

http://www.enslow.com

Original edition published as *Headaches* in 2001.

Library of Congress Cataloging-in-Publication Data
Silverstein, Alvin.
Handy health guide to headaches / by Alvin and Virginia Silverstein and Laura Silverstein Nunn.
pages cm. — (Handy health guides)
  Summary: "Find out what a headache is, what causes them, when you should see a doctor, and how to prevent and
treat them"—Provided by publisher.
Includes bibliographical references and index.
  ISBN 978-0-7660-4277-3
  1. Headache—Juvenile literature. I. Silverstein, Virginia B. II. Nunn, Laura Silverstein. III. Title.
  RC392.S526 2014
  616.8'4913—dc23
                              2012041454

Future editions:
Paperback ISBN: 978-1-4644-0497-9
EPUB ISBN: 978-1-4645-1257-5
Single-User PDF ISBN: 978-1-4646-1257-2
Multi-User PDF ISBN: 978-0-7660-5889-7

Printed in the United States of America

052013 Lake Book Manufacturing, Inc., Melrose Park, IL

10 9 8 7 6 5 4 3 2 1

To Our Readers: We have done our best to make sure all Internet Addresses in this book were active and appropriate
when we went to press. However, the author and the publisher have no control over and assume no liability for the
material available on those Internet sites or on other Web sites they may link to. Any comments or suggestions can be
sent by e-mail to comments@enslow.com or to the address on the back cover.

♻ Enslow Publishers, Inc., is committed to printing our books on recycled paper. The paper in every book contains
10% to 30% post-consumer waste (PCW). The cover board on the outside of each book contains 100% PCW.
Our goal is to do our part to help young people and the environment too!

CONTENTS

Do you ever
have a bad
headache?

1

OH, MY ACHING HEAD!

What a busy day at school! You survived a pop quiz and an exhausting gym class, but then you almost missed the bus! When you get home, you plop down on the cushy sofa, press your hands to your head, and moan, "Oh, my head hurts!" You have a headache.

A headache is a sign that something is wrong in your body. Many things can cause headaches—a tough day at school, certain foods, or the flashing special effects on a TV show. You can even get a headache when you're hungry, or when you don't get enough sleep. Many common illnesses, such as colds and flu, can also cause headaches.

Teens Get Headaches Too!

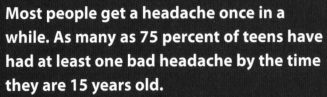

Most people get a headache once in a while. As many as 75 percent of teens have had at least one bad headache by the time they are 15 years old.

Not all headaches are the same. Most are just an annoying dull ache that makes it hard to think. But some are *really* bad. They make you feel like your head is going to explode. The pain may be constant, or it may be throbbing—like a heartbeat.

Headaches can be a real pain, but most are not serious. Sometimes, though, headaches can hurt so much or happen so often that you need to see a doctor. A doctor can help you find out what is causing the headaches. Once you know what the problem is, you can find ways to treat the headaches or get rid of them completely.

2

WHAT IS A HEADACHE?

Headaches are among the most common health problems in the United States. Millions of adults, teens, and kids suffer from headaches. Even young children quickly learn to identify the pain of a hurting head.

When you have a headache, the pain seems to be coming from inside your head. At first you might think your brain is hurt, but that isn't really true. Your brain is the control center for all your thoughts, feelings, and body movements. Information about the world travels from your eyes, ears, nose, mouth, and skin to your brain. These messages are carried by nerves.

When you get hurt, nerves carry pain messages to your brain. But your brain itself does not have nerve endings that can sense pain. If your brain were damaged,

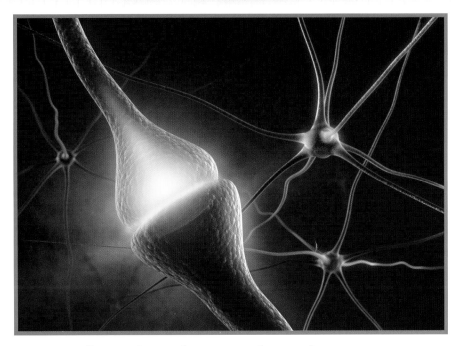

Nerve cells, such as the ones shown here, carry messages to the brain, where they are turned into something we can understand—like pain.

you wouldn't feel any pain. In fact, a doctor can operate on a person's brain while he or she is awake!

So what is it that's hurting when you have a headache? Most of the time, the pain comes from outside the skull, from the nerves, blood vessels, and muscles that cover your head, neck, and scalp. Blood vessels in and around your brain can hurt you too. They may swell up and put pressure on nearby nerves. Nerves in your face, mouth, or throat may also be responsible. When any

Your Brain Feels No Pain

Patients are usually not awake when they have surgery. Imagine how painful it would be if they were! But brain surgery is a different story. Some doctors actually want their patients to be awake during their operation. While poking around the patient's brain, the doctor will talk to the patient and the patient will talk right back! That way if there's a change in the patient's speech, such as slurring or trouble speaking, the doctor will stop before there's any damage.

of these nerves sends pain messages to your brain, you get a headache.

Most people get headaches every once in a while. Some people get headaches more often. They may get a headache several times a week—or even every day. A headache may last for a few minutes, a few hours, or a few days.

Headache pain may be rather mild or really annoying. A bad headache can make you want to just curl up and go to sleep, but sometimes headaches hurt so much that you can't sleep.

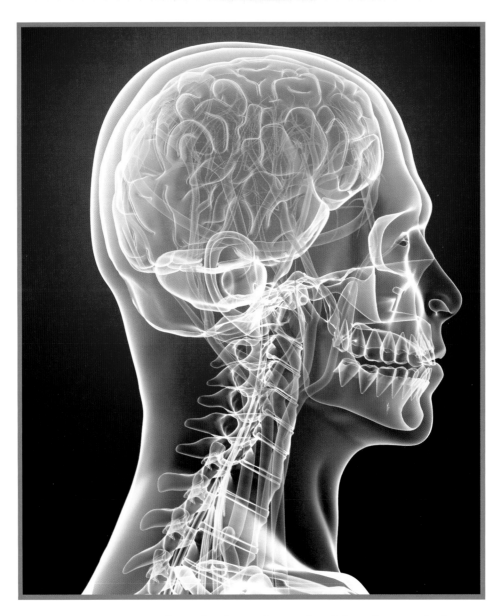

You may get a headache when the blood vessels in your head or neck (red) swell up and press on nearby nerves, sending pain messages to the brain.

Homework has really stressed this person out. Now he feels a headache pain in the back of his head.

There are two main kinds of headaches: tension headaches and migraine headaches. When you have a tension headache, you feel a dull pain that just won't let up. It feels like something is pressing on your head. The pain may be in the front or back of your head or on both sides. Sometimes a tension headache feels like a tight band around your head.

A migraine is a different kind of headache. The pain is sharp and throbbing. And it is usually in just one area.

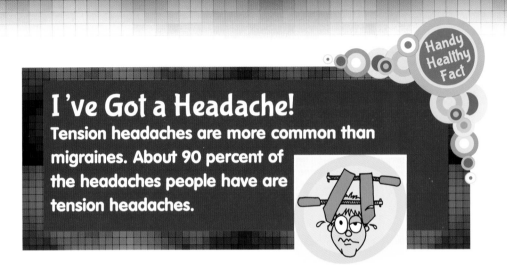

I've Got a Headache!

Tension headaches are more common than migraines. About 90 percent of the headaches people have are tension headaches.

The name *migraine* comes from a Greek word meaning "half a head," because the pain often occurs on just one side of the head. But some migraines make both sides of your head hurt, or the pain may spread from one side to the other. You may also be unusually sensitive to bright light, loud noises, or strong smells.

A migraine is sometimes called a "sick headache" because it can make you feel dizzy or sick to your stomach. You may even throw up.

Some headaches are a combination of both migraine and tension headaches. You may start with a migraine. Then, if the pain makes you tighten muscles in your head and neck, you may end up with a tension headache too. In some situations, a tension headache may also bring on a migraine.

3
WHAT TRIGGERS HEADACHES?

Believe it or not, a headache is actually meant to help you, not hurt you. A headache is your body's way of telling you that something is wrong.

There are a number of different things that can trigger a headache. A change in your everyday activities—such as getting too much or too little sleep—can bring on a headache. So can skipping a meal or eating much later than usual. A very bumpy bus ride can make your head hurt.

You may get a headache when you feel sad, angry, worried, or upset. When you worry about a test at school or troubles at home, your head may start to hurt. You may also develop a headache if you are really upset after a fight with a good friend.

Some people get headaches from strong smells, such as smoke, perfume, a new carpet, or fumes from paint or gasoline. The flickering glare of a TV or computer screen can also trigger a headache. Some people get headaches when they eat certain foods, such as chocolate, cheese, yogurt, citrus fruits, bananas, bacon, bologna, or hot dogs. Caffeine can trigger headaches too. So can food additives, such as NutraSweet and monosodium glutamate (MSG).

It looks like somebody didn't get enough sleep. This can cause a headache.

A mask can help protect you from harmful fumes that could give you a headache.

Headaches that develop after a head injury may be a sign of serious trouble. Normally, your skull protects your brain, but when you hit your head, your brain may crash against your skull. If blood vessels are damaged, they will bleed and swell, causing a painful headache. If you get a headache after falling off your bike or tripping down the stairs, see a doctor right away.

Be sure to wear a helmet when you are riding a bike.
If you fall, the helmet can prevent brain injury.

Brain Freeze

Did you ever get a headache after eating ice cream too quickly? People often call this "brain freeze." When ice cream touches the roof of your mouth, the cold temperature sets off a nerve at the back of your throat, and that causes a head-ache. Ice pops, slushy frozen drinks, or even cold soda, milk, or juice can also give you brain freeze.

Luckily, this kind of headache usually goes away in just a few minutes. If you start to feel brain freeze coming on, try holding your tongue against the roof of your mouth. This will warm the area and may help you avoid the headache. And next time, slow down when you're drinking that slushy!

17

In rare cases, headaches may be caused by a brain tumor. When a tumor grows inside the brain, it pushes normal brain tissues aside and presses against them. Because most brain tissues do not sense pain, the person usually doesn't feel any pain until the tumor is fairly large. As the tumor continues to grow, the headaches gradually get worse and happen more often. If doctors catch a brain tumor early, they may be able to remove it.

Don't Get Stressed!

Teenagers get migraines most often on Mondays and least often on Saturdays. Doctors think the reason is the stress of facing the first day of the school week.

4

ALL ABOUT HEADACHES

When you are watching an interesting TV show or playing an exciting video game, you may not realize that you are sitting in an uncomfortable position. But when the show or game is over, your body aches and your head hurts. You have a full-blown tension headache.

Tension headaches occur when muscles in your face, neck, or scalp tense up, or tighten, for long periods of time. Your muscles may tighten when you are worried about something. Studying hard for a test or watching TV too long can also make your head and neck muscles tighten.

Sitting in an uncomfortable position can give you a headache, but you may not notice the problem until it is too late.

If you have a tension headache, it may be hard to think or pay attention. But this type of headache is not usually serious enough to keep you from doing things—even though you may feel miserable doing them.

Migraines are a different story. A migraine can make you feel so tired that you just want to lie down. Migraines may be so painful that you cannot take part in everyday activities. You may not even want to get up and walk around

You are more likely to get migraines if one of your parents, grandparents, aunts, uncles, or some other family member gets them. If one of your parents gets migraines, there's a 50 percent chance that you will

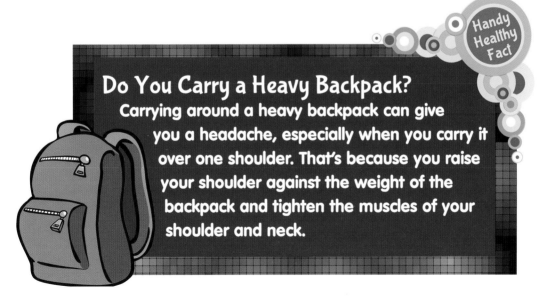

Handy Healthy Fact

Do You Carry a Heavy Backpack?

Carrying around a heavy backpack can give you a headache, especially when you carry it over one shoulder. That's because you raise your shoulder against the weight of the backpack and tighten the muscles of your shoulder and neck.

get them. If both of your parents get migraines, you have a 75 percent chance of getting them.

There are two main kinds of migraines—migraines with aura and migraines without aura. A person who has a migraine with aura may sense when a headache is coming on. During a period called the prodrome, the person may feel sad, crabby, moody, or restless. Some people become forgetful or have trouble speaking. Others lose their appetite, yawn a lot, or become sensitive to lights, sounds, and smells. All these things are like warning signs that can develop hours before the actual headache.

Alice in Wonderland

The British writer Lewis Carroll often suffered from migraines. His auras were quite unusual. Instead of flashing zigzags, he had hallucinations. He saw and heard things that weren't there! Carroll based many of the unusual incidents in his famous book *Alice's Adventures in Wonderland* on his strange hallucinations.

Activity 1:
The Pulses in Your Head

Has a doctor or nurse ever taken your pulse? He or she was timing your heartbeat by feeling the throbbing beat on the inside of your wrist, where an artery passes close to the surface. You can also feel a person's pulse by pressing against the large blood vessels on the sides of the neck or the forehead.

Try to find all these pulse points on yourself and a friend. Look at a watch or clock with a second hand and count the number of beats per minute. What is your pulse? Is your friend's higher or lower? Adults normally have a pulse rate of about 70, but a child's pulse beats faster. Exercise and excitement can also make your pulse speed up.

Shortly before the headache starts, a person having a migraine with aura may experience some really weird things. Some people start to see bright flashing lights and quivering, zigzagging lines. During this period, which doctors call the aura, people may also feel numbness and pins and needles—especially in their lips or hands. If they try to read, it may seem like words are missing from some parts of the page. People may even have trouble talking or experience muscle weakness. The aura usually lasts for about ten to thirty minutes.

Migraine pain usually starts once the aura goes away. During the headache, any kind of movement makes migraine pain worse. Even after the headache pain stops, the person may still have some of the symptoms and feel "wiped out."

Only about 10 to 20 percent of people who get migraines experience an aura. The rest have migraines without aura. They have no obvious warning signs, but the headache is just as bad. There may also be nausea, vomiting, dizziness, and the other typical migraine symptoms.

Medical experts say that migraines result from changes in the level of certain chemicals in the brain, especially a substance called serotonin. Serotonin helps nerves carry messages from one part of the brain to another. This chemical controls your mood, how well you sleep, and the widening or narrowing of your blood vessels.

A migraine may begin when a person is exposed to bright flashing lights, feels worried or upset, or eats certain foods. These triggers cause the amount of serotonin in the person's brain to increase. Then blood vessels become narrow, or constrict.

The brain normally receives a rich supply of blood. The blood is full of oxygen and sugar to power the body's activities. When blood vessels constrict, important parts of the brain do not get enough blood. Then a person may see flashing lights or feel dizzy or numb, or have other aura symptoms.

The migraine does not stop there. Serotonin leaks out of the blood vessels into the surrounding tissues, lowering the amount of serotonin in the brain. The lack of serotonin makes it easier for other sense messages to get through. That is probably why people with migraines are often very sensitive to light, noise, and smells. The lack of serotonin also causes blood vessels in the head to

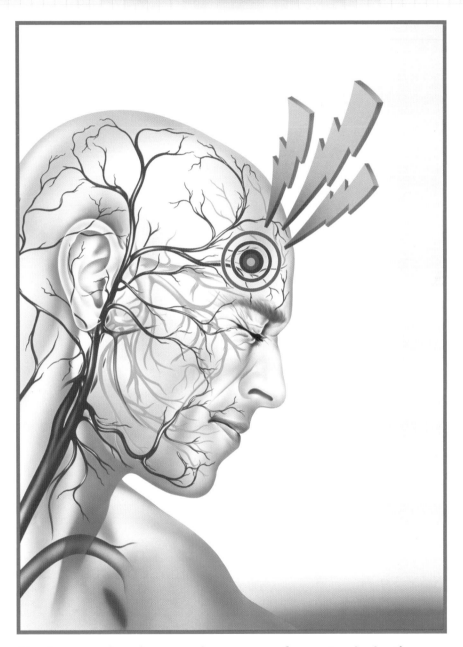

During a migraine, an increase of serotonin in the
brain causes blood vessels to swell up.

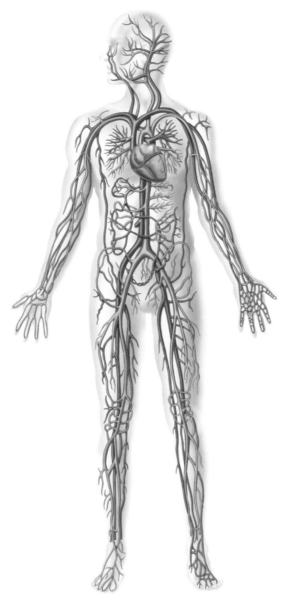

Arteries (in red) carry oxygen-rich blood from the heart to all parts of the body.

swell and widen, or dilate. The swollen blood vessels press on nearby nerves, and the painful part of the headache begins.

Why does migraine pain throb? It seems almost like a heartbeat. Actually, it is a reflection of the heart's beating. Your heart is a pump. The strong muscles in its walls contract (tighten) in a steady rhythm, pushing blood into a network of arteries that carry it to every part of your body. After each heartbeat—as a surge of blood gushes through the arteries—muscles in the walls of your arteries contract too. This helps keep your blood moving through your body. That rhythmic pumping produces the throbbing a person feels during a migraine.

Eventually the swollen blood vessels return to normal and the migraine eases. Sometimes vomiting or falling asleep can help to end a migraine. After "sleeping it off," a person may wake up feeling refreshed and full of energy. But sometimes feelings of tiredness and listlessness—the migraine "hangover"—may drag on for a day or two.

5

WHEN TO SEE A DOCTOR

Although millions of people get headaches, doctors don't usually hear about them. Most headaches occur just once in a while and can be treated by pain relievers sold in stores. These headaches do not usually send people rushing to the doctor. But if you get headaches often, or if they make it hard for you to live normally, then it's time to seek medical help.

A doctor may be able to help you find out what's causing your headaches. Then you can decide

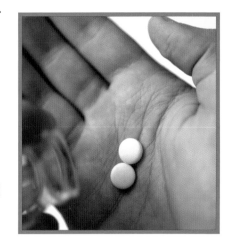

Aspirin is often used for treating headaches, but children and teens under the age of 18 should not take aspirin.

what kind of treatment you need. A doctor will also know whether your headaches are a sign of a more serious illness.

First, the doctor will ask you some questions about your headaches. The doctor will want to know when the headaches started, when and how often they occur, how long they last, and which parts of your head hurt. Is the pain dull or sharp, mild or severe, throbbing or constant? Do the headaches start after you eat a certain food, look at a bright light, or when you get upset or stressed? Does the pain get worse when you bend over, cough, sneeze, strain, or move your head suddenly? Do you have problems sleeping?

The doctor will also ask whether you get any warning signs that a headache is coming, such as spots, flashing lights, or zigzags before the eyes. Do you experience nausea and vomiting or sensitivity to light, noise, or smells? Have you had any head injuries, serious illnesses, or surgery for a tumor or a brain disease? Do any of your close relatives have migraines or other headache problems? Your answers to these questions will help the doctor figure out what is causing your headaches.

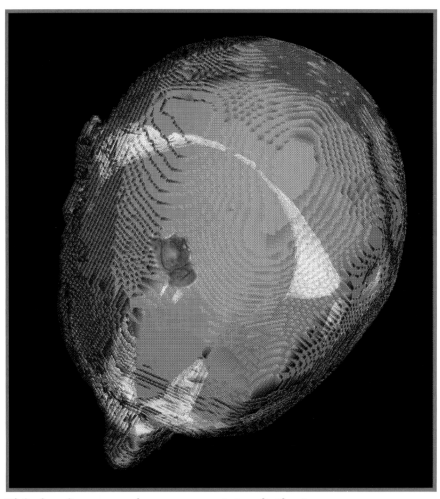

This brain scan shows a cyst (red) that may grow larger and cause painful headaches.

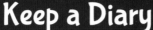

Keep a Diary

It's a good idea to keep a diary of your headaches. Write down the date and time of each headache. Describe what each headache feels like and what you were doing when you got it. These notes can help you remember important details. By looking at a few weeks of your headache records, the doctor may be able to spot a pattern and discover clues to your problem.

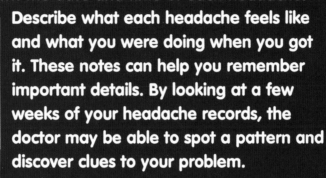

A complete physical exam can provide additional information. For instance, your headaches may be due to eyestrain. An eye test may show that you need glasses.

If the doctor thinks that the headaches may indicate a more serious problem, you may be given some other tests. A CT scan or MRI scan produces revealing pictures of the brain. These tests can show tumors, cysts, or other problems. Once the doctor figures out what kind of headaches you've been having, you can start treating them.

6

TREATING HEADACHES

Many people treat their headaches themselves, without going to a doctor. They take a pain reliever, such as acetaminophen, ibuprofen, or naproxen. These drugs are popular because they are usually quick and effective. They are also safe enough to take without a doctor's prescription.

How do pain-relieving drugs work? When body cells or tissues are damaged, they release a chemical called prostaglandin. This chemical stimulates the nerves that send pain messages to the brain. Aspirin and other pain relievers prevent cells from releasing prostaglandin. When your brain stops getting pain messages, your headache disappears. Ibuprofen and naproxen also help reduce swelling. (Acetaminophen, though, does not reduce swelling.) Some pain medicines contain caffeine.

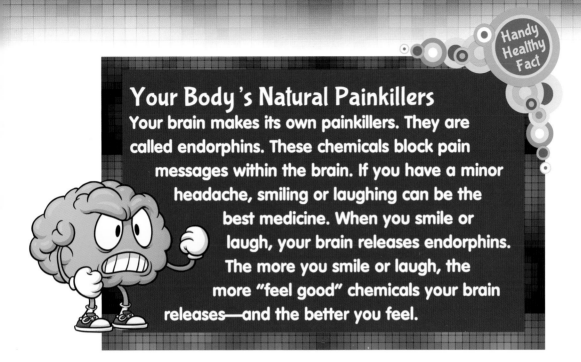

Your Body's Natural Painkillers

Your brain makes its own painkillers. They are called endorphins. These chemicals block pain messages within the brain. If you have a minor headache, smiling or laughing can be the best medicine. When you smile or laugh, your brain releases endorphins. The more you smile or laugh, the more "feel good" chemicals your brain releases—and the better you feel.

Caffeine helps the pain-relieving drugs work better in the body. It also makes blood vessels constrict, which may help relieve migraine headaches. But too much caffeine can cause a headache!

While you're waiting for a pain reliever to work, you can help a tension headache by napping, rubbing your head and neck muscles, putting a hot compress or an ice pack where it hurts, or taking a hot bath. You may be able to ease a migraine headache by lying down in a dark, quiet room.

People who get migraines with aura may be able to avoid pain if they pay attention to the warning signs.

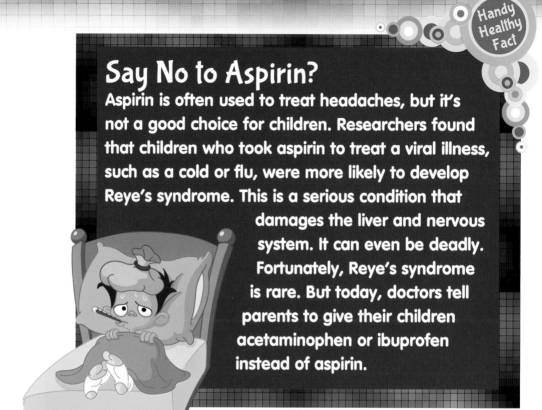

Say No to Aspirin?

Aspirin is often used to treat headaches, but it's not a good choice for children. Researchers found that children who took aspirin to treat a viral illness, such as a cold or flu, were more likely to develop Reye's syndrome. This is a serious condition that damages the liver and nervous system. It can even be deadly. Fortunately, Reye's syndrome is rare. But today, doctors tell parents to give their children acetaminophen or ibuprofen instead of aspirin.

Taking a combination of a pain reliever and caffeine at the first hint of flashing lights or numbness can block the pain messages before they get to the brain.

Headaches may be a sign of stress at school or at home. Your body may respond to these strong feelings by giving you frequent headaches. If this happens, you may want to see a counselor. A counselor can help you get to the root of the problem and deal with it. Eventually, as you overcome your problem, the headaches should lessen or go away completely.

Can a counselor help this girl figure out why she gets so many headaches?

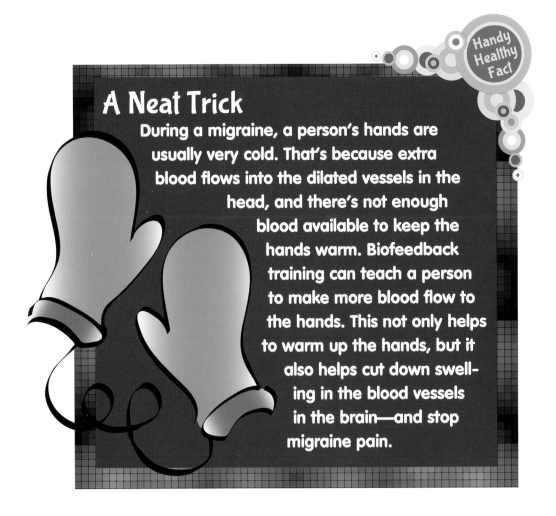

A Neat Trick

During a migraine, a person's hands are usually very cold. That's because extra blood flows into the dilated vessels in the head, and there's not enough blood available to keep the hands warm. Biofeedback training can teach a person to make more blood flow to the hands. This not only helps to warm up the hands, but it also helps cut down swelling in the blood vessels in the brain—and stop migraine pain.

Biofeedback is often an effective way to treat people who get a lot of headaches. In biofeedback, electrodes are attached to various parts of the body. They track and monitor temperature, muscle activity, and heart rate. By watching the tracking instruments while practicing relaxing techniques, a person can learn how to control some of the body's reactions to stress.

People who learn how to relax their muscles can sometimes prevent tension headaches before they start. And some people can even stop their migraines by learning how to reduce blood flow to the scalp. This technique prevents arteries in the person's head from throbbing. After practicing with biofeedback electrodes, many people can often stop headaches without using drugs.

7

PREVENTING HEADACHES

There are a number of safe and simple things you can do on your own to lower your risk of getting headaches. If you know what kinds of things give you headaches, try to stay away from them. For instance, if you notice that you get headaches after eating bacon or hot dogs, don't eat those foods.

You can also avoid getting a headache by sticking to a daily routine. A healthy body needs a good night's sleep and enough energy to keep it going all day. So get to bed on time and don't skip meals or wait too long to eat.

You may get a headache when you watch TV or play computer games for a long time. Take frequent breaks. Just gaze into space and chill out, or get up and move around.

Stay away from foods that may give you a headache. Eating the right foods will keep your body healthy.

Taking frequent breaks can keep your eyes from getting overworked.

Stress is a common headache trigger. Everybody gets stressed from time to time. It is not easy to avoid, but you can learn how to relieve it. Taking slow, deep breaths can help release tension. This can prevent your muscles from tightening, and may keep a tension headache from starting. Meditation also helps lower the heart rate and blood pressure and reduces stress. Using your imagination

Handy
Healthy
Fact

Activity 2:
How Common Are Headaches?

You can find out just how common headaches are by taking a survey of your friends and relatives. What kind of headaches do they get? Compare the number of people who get tension headaches to those who get migraines. Try to include people of different ages and both sexes. Ask each one the following questions:

- Have you ever had a headache? If so, how often?
- What do your headaches feel like? Do you get the dull, constant pain of a tension headache, or the painful throbbing of a migraine?
- Where is the pain? Do you get different kinds of headaches?
- Do you know what causes your headaches?
- How do you ease the pain of a headache? Do pain relievers help, or do you need to go to the doctor?

Look over the results carefully. Do you find that adults get more headaches than children? Do they occur more in one sex than the other? What other interesting things have you discovered?

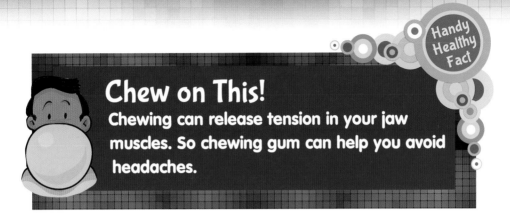

to create a soothing picture in your mind can help you to relax, too.

When you run and jump and get plenty of regular exercise, your brain makes extra endorphins. These natural chemicals can help you avoid headaches. You can also do exercises to relax the muscles in your neck, shoulders, jaw, and back.

You may not be able to completely avoid getting headaches, but following these good health practices will make them much less likely to happen.

GLOSSARY

artery—One of the large blood vessels that carry blood from the heart to the rest of the body.

aura—A warning period shortly before a migraine headache. Warning signs include flashing lights; bright, zigzag lines; blind spots; and numbness or a feeling of pins and needles in the lips or hands.

biofeedback—A method of learning how to control certain body processes, including temperature, blood pressure, and muscle tension.

blood vessel—One of the tubes that carry blood throughout the body.

caffeine—A chemical that stimulates the body and causes blood vessels to constrict.

constrict—To become narrow.

contract—To tighten.

CT scan—Also CAT (computerized axial tomography) scan, a test in which X-rays are sent through the body at various angles to examine soft tissues.

cyst—A fluid-filled growth that forms in the body.

dilate—To widen.

endorphins—Chemicals in the body that act as natural painkillers.

hallucination—A mental state in which a person sees and hears things that are not there.

migraine—A severe, throbbing headache that occurs when blood vessels to the brain become narrow and then widen. The pain is usually felt on one side of the head. Other symptoms such as nausea and vomiting often accompany the headache.

MRI scan—A picture of body tissues created by an imaging technique called magnetic resonance imaging.

nerves—Structures that carry messages to and from the brain.

prodrome—A warning period up to twenty-four hours before a migraine headache begins. Warning signs may include sadness, irritability, restlessness, mood swings, speech or memory problems, a loss of appetite, or sensitivity to lights, sounds, and smells.

prostaglandin—A chemical in the body that stimulates nerve endings that send pain messages to the brain.

Reye's syndrome—A rare but serious illness that is associated with taking aspirin during an illness caused by a virus.

scalp—The skin on top of your head. It is usually covered with hair.

serotonin—A chemical in the brain that controls a person's sleep habits, and the narrowing and widening of blood vessels.

tension headache—A dull, constant pain caused when muscles in the face, neck, and scalp tighten for a long period of time.

tumor—A cluster of rapidly growing cells. Some tumors are cancerous.

LEARN MORE

Books

Brown, Anne K. *Migraines*. Detroit: Lucent Books, 2010.

Cobb, Allan B. *Frequently Asked Questions About Migraines and Headaches*. New York: Rosen Publishing Group, 2008.

Goldsmith, Connie. *Neurological Disorders*. Woodbridge, Conn.: Blackbirch Press, 2001.

Parker, Steve. *The Brain and Nervous System*. Chicago: Raintree, 2004.

Petreycik, Rick. *Headaches*. Tarrytown, N.Y.: Benchmark Books, 2006.

LEARN MORE

Web Sites

TeensHealth from Nemours: Migraine Headaches
<http://kidshealth.org/teen/diseases_conditions/ brain_nervous/migraines.html>

University of Washington. Neuroscience for Kids.
<http://faculty.washington.edu/chudler/introb. html#di>

INDEX

INDEX

N

napping, 33
nerves, 7, 8–9, 24, 27, 32
noise, 12, 24, 29
numbness, 23, 24, 34

P

pain, 6, 7–9, 11, 12, 14, 18, 23, 27, 28, 29, 32, 33, 34, 36, 40
pain relievers, 28, 32–33, 34, 39, 40
physical exam, 31
position of the body, 20
preventing headaches, 37, 38–39, 41

prodrome, 21
prostaglandin, 32

S

scalp, 8, 19, 37
school, 5, 13, 18, 34
serotonin, 24, 27
sleep, 5, 9, 13, 24, 27, 29, 38
smells, 12, 14, 21, 24, 29
stress, 18, 29, 34, 37, 39

T

television, 5, 14, 19, 38
treatment, 6, 28, 29, 31, 32–34, 37
tumor, 18, 29, 31

types of headaches, 19–20
  migraine, 11, 12, 18, 20–21, 23–24, 27, 29, 33, 36, 37, 40
  tension, 11, 12, 19–20, 33, 37, 39, 40